Arnav Sharma's *Bloodline's Revenge* opens with excitement, blending adventure and mystery through its youthful characters. The narrative focuses on two brothers, Arnav and Shubh, who are drawn into thrilling situations that test their courage, intelligence, and teamwork. Set in a combination of familiar family dynamics and unexpected challenges, the story follows their journey as they transition from city life to a village, where they face both everyday struggles and extraordinary mysteries.

The central characters—Arnav, a fifteen-year-old with a sharp mind and adventurous spirit, and Shubh, his older brother with a strong, protective nature—must adapt to their new surroundings. The rural backdrop contrasts sharply with the bustling city life they are used to, providing them with new opportunities to learn, grow, and, more importantly, solve the mysterious events that unfold.

Throughout the novel, the brothers encounter strange warnings, eerie settings, and new responsibilities, all while maintaining their youthful optimism and determination to overcome the odds. Their bond as brothers, along with their budding detective skills, serves as the core of the story, giving readers a glimpse into their unique world of adventures.

Young Detectives offers an engaging mix of suspense, lighthearted moments, and the thrill of discovery, without delving into its intricate plot twists. The story explores themes of family, responsibility, and bravery, making it an entertaining and thought-provoking read.

Bloodline's Revenge
The Discovery of Unknown

BY

ARNAV SHARMA

Contents

Young Detectives

"Jump! Jump now!!" The boy screamed.

The boy leaped from the high wall, his energy propelling him through the air as he aimed for the man below. With a thud, he tackled the unsuspecting figure, sending both crashing to the ground. The man let out a surprised grunt as he hit the ground, and the boy, now pinning him, looked exhilarated by his daring move.

"Gotcha!" the boy shouted, a triumphant grin spreading across his face. "The police have been looking for you for ages. Shubh, grab that rope and bind him up. We'll take him to the old mansion—it's the perfect spot. I'm calling the cops right now!"

Shubh, a sixteen-year-old with a muscular build, stood six feet tall, his dusky skin contrasting with his blonde hair and piercing brown eyes. He effortlessly hoisted the man onto his shoulder, carrying him with ease toward the abandoned house. Meanwhile, Arnav, a fifteen-year-old with a slim frame and standing at 5'11", had dark, curly hair and warm brown eyes set against his wheatish complexion. He quickly dialed the police, directing them to the location of the old mansion.

The policeman raised an eyebrow, a hint of curiosity in his voice. "How come it's always you two who end up finding the burglars?"

Arnav, with a proud grin, replied, "We're adventure seekers, sir, dedicated to solving mysteries and catching thieves."

The officer chuckled, clearly impressed. "You two are going to be excellent detectives when you grow up. I hope you stay safe and keep up the good work. See you next time with more burglars to catch!"

The boys smiled, their enthusiasm undiminished. "Thank you, sir! We'll see you next time," they replied in unison, sharing a look of satisfaction.

Bad Starting

"Grandma, can I have something to eat, please?" Arnav asked, his stomach growling.

"Of course, dear. What would you like?" his grandmother replied warmly. "Hmm, maybe a samosa… but that might take a while. Would you mind just giving me some milk and cereal instead?" Arnav asked, a bit unsure. "Sure, honey," his grandmother said with a reassuring smile. "Just give me a minute to warm up the milk for you."

After finishing his meal, Arnav headed upstairs to study. About an hour later, his grandfather called out, "Arnav, come here. I need to talk to you."

Arnav quickly made his way downstairs, a sense of urgency in his steps. He knew all too well the consequences of ignoring his grandfather's calls.

When Arnav walked into the drawing room, he noticed papers scattered across the table, and both his elder brother Shubh and their grandmother were already there. Shubh's usually relaxed demeanor was replaced by a look of frustration. Their grandfather was seated at the head of the table, and he motioned for Arnav to sit down.

"I have some important news," their grandfather began, his tone serious. "I've been transferred to Delhi for work, so your grandmother and I will be moving there."

Arnav's heart sank. "And what about us?" he asked, trying to keep his voice steady despite the uncertainty creeping in. "You two will be going to a local school in a village near Uppada, Andhra Pradesh" their grandfather explained, his expression stern but kind. Arnav's eyebrows knitted together in confusion. "But why can't we live with you and Grandma?". Their grandmother, her face soft with concern, chimed in,

"You've spent eight or nine years studying in the city. It's important for you to experience life in a village, too. It will be a valuable experience."

"But…" Arnav started, feeling a wave of frustration and disappointment. Before he could continue, his grandfather cut him off. "Enough, Arnav," his grandfather said firmly. "This decision is final. You and Shubh will be moving to the village school. Now, it's time for you to accept it. Finish your dinner, and then start packing your things. We leave tomorrow."

Arnav looked at Shubh, who gave him a sympathetic glance. He could see the mix of emotions in his brother's eyes, reflecting his own turmoil. Arnav wanted to protest, but the finality in his grandfather's voice made it clear that there was no room for negotiation.

As the family gathered for dinner, Arnav's mind raced with thoughts of what awaited them in the village. He knew that no amount of arguing would change the situation, so he focused on finishing his meal and mentally preparing for the new chapter in their lives. After dinner, he and Shubh began the task of packing their belongings, trying to make sense of the sudden change and the adventure that lay ahead.

"What a stupid reason is that" said Arnav with anger. "How are we going to survive in a hostel which is in a village and that also without electronics, all we'll get is a nineties telephone to talk to our grandparents" said Shubh sadly. They stuffed everything they got, in their bags then went to their bed to sleep.

Arnav barely slept, his anxiety keeping him awake for most of the night. When the first light of dawn crept through the curtains, he reluctantly got up and began preparing for their departure. His mind was a whirl of emotions—nervousness, excitement, and a tinge of dread. Shubh, on the other hand, had overslept and was in a frantic rush. The clamor of hurried footsteps and the sound of items being tossed into bags filled the house as Shubh scrambled to get ready.

"Are you ready, brother?" Arnav called out, trying to inject some enthusiasm into his voice to lift Shubh's spirits, even though he, too, was feeling apprehensive about the move.

Shubh, his face showing a mix of frustration and resignation, replied, "This is a terrible start to class eleven."

Arnav, trying to be optimistic, said, "Come on, bro, I'll be starting class ten, and I'm sure we'll have fun. It'll be an adventure!"

Shubh sighed, his shoulders slumping. "Yeah, sure… I hope so," he said, his voice laced with grief and uncertainty.

Despite the gloomy mood, Arnav grabbed his bag and gave his brother a reassuring pat on the back. "We'll make the best of it. Let's get going. We've got a new place to explore and new experiences ahead."

With that, the two brothers headed out, the weight of the unknown ahead but the hope of making the most of their new circumstances driving them forward.

Knocked Out

The family had arranged for a shipping agency to transport their belongings to Delhi via a truck, leaving only Arnav and Shubh to carry their personal bags in the family's car. As the truck began its journey toward the city, the family set off in their Xcent, heading towards their new destination.

The highways stretched out before them, remarkably clear for the time of day. The landscape was picturesque, with lush green trees lining the road and the occasional glimpse of distant fields. The drive was long but pleasant, the serene beauty of the countryside offering a welcome distraction from the tension of the move.

The Xcent, with its comfortable seats and smooth ride, helped ease the journey. Six hours passed quickly, with the rhythm of the road and the changing scenery making the time feel shorter. As they approached the village, the first signs of rural life began to appear, and the familiar cityscape gave way to open fields and small, quaint houses.

When they finally arrived, the village greeted them with its own unique charm. The slower pace of life, the warm sun, and the simplicity of the surroundings were a stark contrast to the bustling city they were leaving behind. The brothers took a deep breath, ready to embrace their new home and the experiences that awaited them in this tranquil setting.

But the reality of their new surroundings quickly set in. Unlike the smooth, paved roads they were accustomed to, the village roads were unmetalled and rough. They parked their car near the entrance of the village and began their walk to the school.

The path they took was narrow and uneven, with an open drainage system running alongside it. The unpleasant odor from the open drains made the already challenging trek even less enjoyable. The road, far from being the main thoroughfare, was in poor condition, adding to the discomfort of carrying their heavy bags.

As they trudged along, the brothers' frustration grew. The road they were on seemed to stretch endlessly, and the heavy weight of their bags felt increasingly burdensome. Just as they were resigning themselves to the arduous journey, they noticed a broader road in the distance, which appeared to be in much better condition.

To their dismay, it became evident that this wider, smoother road was the main route into the village—the one they could have used to drive their car closer to the school. The realization only intensified their irritation as they had to carry their bags much further than necessary.

Shubh, already in a bad mood, grumbled under his breath while Arnav tried to stay positive despite the inconvenience. The brothers exchanged exasperated glances, their earlier optimism dampened by the unexpected challenges of their new environment. They continued on, determined to reach their destination.

The grandparents, unfamiliar with the village layout, were unsure of the way to the local school. Their grandfather approached a man sitting outside his modest home, hoping for directions.

"Excuse me, sir," he called out, "can you please tell us how to get to the village's local school?"

The man looked up with an unsettling expression, his eyes shadowed by the brim of his hat. He made an eerie gesture toward a nearby path. "The school? It's... it's about a kilometer from here if you take that turn," he said, his voice wavering. "But I must warn you—don't go down the old road. Many have died... many. It's not safe. People say the place is haunted, the house of ghosts. The stories are not just tales; you should be careful."

The grandfather's face tightened in concern, but he nodded

appreciatively. "Thank you for the warning. We'll take the main route."

With that, the family turned toward the road indicated by the man, cautiously making their way toward the school. The ominous warning lingered in their minds as they proceeded, each step echoing the unease stirred by the stranger's cryptic words.

The grandparents exchanged a glance, their expressions reflecting skepticism. Clearly, they didn't take the stranger's warning seriously and decided to follow the route he had indicated.

As they walked, the grandfather, still uncertain, stopped another man heading in the opposite direction to confirm their path. "Hello, my friend," he asked, trying to stay polite despite the mounting anxiety. "Can you tell us if this road leads to the local school?"

The man's reaction was unsettling. He stopped abruptly, his face paling as he spoke. "Don't, don't go that way. It's no good... people died there, and now... now they kill." With a hurried, fearful glance, he turned and walked away, leaving a trail of unease in his wake.

Arnav and Shubh exchanged frightened looks, their minds racing with thoughts of the eerie warnings they had just received. The idea that the place was associated with death and danger was unsettling.

However, their grandfather, trying to maintain a sense of normalcy and dismissing the villagers' ominous warnings, said, "Don't worry about it. The villagers are just a bunch of crooks with wild tales. We're going the right way."

Determined to proceed despite their growing apprehension, the family continued along the path the man had described. Each step felt heavier as they ventured deeper into the unknown, their earlier excitement overshadowed by the unsettling rumors. The village seemed to grow quieter, the only sounds being their footsteps and the distant calls of unfamiliar birds, as they made their way toward the school.

After walking for some time, the family finally spotted a sign that indicated the school was nearby. A wave of relief washed over them as they approached the school's entrance.

When they arrived, the grandparents turned to Arnav and Shubh. "You two go inside," their grandfather instructed. "You've already been enrolled, so just head on in."

The grandmother, her eyes moist with emotion, hugged the boys tightly. "Goodbye, children. Grandma will miss both of you so much," she said, her voice breaking with sadness.

"We'll make sure to pay your fees every month," their grandfather added, his tone firm but caring. "Just stay within the school premises and don't wander around this strange village."

Arnav looked up, a mix of hope and concern in his eyes. "Wouldn't you at least come in to introduce us to the principal?"

Their grandfather shook his head apologetically. "I have to report to my office as soon as possible, my boy. I'm afraid I can't stay."

With one last, heartfelt hug and a few encouraging words, the grandparents said their final goodbyes. As they watched their grandparents drive away, Arnav and Shubh stood at the threshold of the school, the weight of their new reality settling in. The school loomed ahead, a symbol of their fresh start in this unfamiliar village, and they braced themselves for the next chapter of their lives.

"Weren't they acting weird?" asked Arnav. "Yes, it's our first day, at least they should have introduced to our principal." Shubh replied.

 As Arnav and Shubh entered the school's main gate, they were confronted by a tall, slender boy with a deep brown complexion, brown hair, and piercing black eyes. He stood directly in their path, blocking their way.

"Were those your grandparents?" the boy asked, pointing toward the distant figure of their grandparents as they drove away.

"Yes, do you have a problem with that—" Arnav started to respond, but his sentence was abruptly cut off when the boy landed a punch squarely on his face. The force of the blow knocked Arnav out cold, and he crumpled to the ground.

Shubh's eyes widened in shock and fury. "What the—how dare you, you idiot!" he roared, launching himself at the attacker. The two boys grappled fiercely, Shubh's anger fueling his strength. After a brief struggle, Shubh managed to throw the boy to the ground and began kicking him.

At that moment, two other boys ran over, joining the fray. One of them delivered a punch to Shubh's stomach, causing him to double over. The other boy took advantage of Shubh's compromised position and kicked him in the face. Shubh collapsed, and both boys started to pummel him mercilessly.

Just as the situation seemed to spiral out of control, a group of students rushed in to break up the fight. A teacher arrived on the scene quickly, assessing the chaos. Without hesitation, he took Arnav and Shubh to the Principal's office, with the boys still reeling from the confrontation.

Before leading the brothers away, the teacher turned to the aggressor. "Saransh, this is the first time you've disrupted the school's discipline. I'm letting you off this time, but don't let it happen again."

The teacher then addressed Arnav and Shubh, his tone stern but concerned. "You two are new here, right?"

"Yes, sir," they replied in unison, still shaken from the ordeal.

The teacher nodded, his expression softening slightly. "This will be the first and last time you get into a fight here. If it happens again, you'll be expelled immediately."

He then turned to Shubh, who was still seething with anger. "What started this fight, exactly?"

Shubh, catching his breath, explained, "It wasn't our fault, sir. Saransh just asked us about our grandparents, then he punched Arnav out of nowhere."

The teacher listened intently, taking note of their account. "I'll look into this further," he said, guiding them into the principal's office. "For now, let's get you both settled and ensure this doesn't escalate any further."

As they entered the Principal's office, the teacher motioned for them to take a seat after receiving a nod from the Principal.

"Good morning, sir," Arnav and Shubh greeted in unison.

"Good morning," the Principal replied, his gaze shifting to the two boys. "You must be the grandsons of Mr. and Mrs. Sharma, correct?"

"Yes, sir," Shubh responded.

The Principal nodded approvingly. "Your grandparents are among the few who choose to send their children here to contribute to the community. It's very kind of them."

Arnav and Shubh exchanged puzzled looks as the Principal continued. "You both have a significant responsibility ahead of you. Apart from your studies, you'll be expected to help the villagers, earn money, and cover your own school fees. It's crucial that you remain determined and hardworking."

Arnav's eyes widened in disbelief. "We'll have to work to pay the fees? Are you serious? How are we supposed to balance schoolwork with working for the villagers? I'm in class 10th, and Shubh is in class 11th. This seems impossible."

The Principal's expression remained steady. "If you had concerns about this arrangement, you should have discussed them with your grandparents. However, it's the reality you're facing now."

He then handed them several documents. "Here are your books, notebooks, and timetables. And this," he said, handing them another sheet, "contains details about your classes."

The Principal continued, "These are your hostel keys. Your accommodation is just behind this building. Settle in, and remember to report to the school from tomorrow. We expect you to adjust quickly and start fulfilling your responsibilities."

As the boys gathered their supplies and keys, the weight of their new reality began to sink in. The Principal's words about balancing school with work and community service loomed over them as they headed toward their new hostel, bracing themselves for the challenges that lay ahead.

What's Happening

"What's happening bro!" shouted Arnav while walking to his hostel with Shubh. "Why didn't our grandparents told us before, that we have to earn for our own! They told us that they'll ensure to pay the fees on time" Arnav was distressed.

As the two brothers crossed the threshold into their school hostels.

They saw that the room they got was on the first floor and was very cozy, even though it was near the graveyard behind the village school hostel. Sunlight peeked through the curtains, making the old wooden floor look warm. They had two single beds with colourful quilts that reminded them of home. Simple desks stood by the wall, waiting for their books and pens. Despite the graveyard nearby, the room felt safe, like a quiet place where they could relax and study. But one thing the two boys noticed was that there was a small trap door near a big three because of which it was difficult to notice from the ground level. Most of the students lived on the front side of the hostel as there weren't many of students so they choose one from where not must sun warmth came and the room remains cool.

Later that evening, Arnav and Shubh ventured out of the school, determined to find a job to help cover their school fees. As they walked through the village, they came across the same man they had met earlier, who was now standing in front of a timber cutting area. The brothers approached him, hoping he could offer them some work.

"We're looking for a job to help pay our school fees," Arnav said. "We heard you might be able to help."

The man, who they now realized was the owner of the timber plot, looked them over carefully. "I can give you both a job, but it's going to be hard work," he warned. "You need to be determined."

"We're up for it," Shubh replied. "When do we start?"

"Come here every day from 6:00 p.m. to 8:00 p.m.," the owner said. "You'll be paid daily."

Arnav glanced at Shubh, who nodded in agreement. "We're in," Arnav said.

The brothers thanked the man and headed back to their hostel. The job seemed like a tough but necessary step, and they were ready to face the challenges it would bring.

As they walked back, their minds were occupied with the new job and the daunting tasks ahead. Suddenly, the scene took a terrifying turn. The same man from earlier appeared out of nowhere, leaping directly in front of Arnav. With a look of horror on his face, he grabbed Arnav by the collar.

"You! You're still alive? But that day he himself killed you! This isn't possible... you're a ghost!!! AAAHHHH!!!" The man screamed, his voice filled with panic. He released Arnav's collar and fled, shouting at the top of his lungs.

Arnav and Shubh stood frozen for a moment, their hearts racing. The man's bizarre reaction had left them stunned and frightened. As the man's footsteps faded into the distance, Shubh quickly grabbed Arnav's hand.

"Come on, let's get out of here," he urged, his voice urgent.

They hurried back to their hostel, their minds reeling from the encounter. The eerie warning from the man, combined with their new job and the strange events of the day, left them both anxious and unsettled as they made their way to the safety of their new home.

Let's Have Some Fun

As some days passes by, they become familiar to their new routine.

One day in the dimly lit halls of their village school, Arnav and Shubh found themselves alone, their classmates having departed for the day. The sun dipped below the horizon, casting long shadows through the windows, and the school seemed to take on a life of its own.

"Arnav," Shubh's voice echoed in the empty corridor, "what are we going to do now? Everyone's gone home, and we're stuck here."

Arnav glanced around, a mischievous glint in his eye. "Maybe we can explore the school or something," he suggested. "It's kinda creepy being here all alone though."

Shubh hesitated, then nodded. "Yeah, but it's also kinda cool. We've got the whole place to ourselves. We can do whatever we want!"

Bolstered by their newfound freedom, the brothers decided to venture into the school's library. With a flashlight in hand, Arnav led the way, illuminating the dusty shelves and rows of books.

"Whoa, look at all these books!" Shubh exclaimed, running his fingers along the spines. "I didn't know we had so many."

Arnav grinned, picking up an old, leather-bound tome. "Yeah, and some of them look really old. Hey, check this out. It's a book about the history of our village."

Intrigued, Shubh joined his brother on the floor as they flipped through the pages, uncovering tales of times long past.

"Did you know there used to be a castle here?" Arnav exclaimed, his eyes widening with excitement.

Shubh shook his head in disbelief. "No way! I had no idea. This is awesome."

As the night wore on, the brothers delved deeper into the book, their imaginations running wild with thoughts of ancient castles and forgotten legends.

"Hey, maybe we can find the ruins of the castle in our summer holidays and explore them," Arnav suggested, breaking the silence.

Shubh's face lit up with anticipation. "That would be amazing! We could be like real-life adventurers."

With plans for their adventure already forming in their minds, the brothers reluctantly closed the book and made their way back to the hostel.

After this as they were walking to their hostel another idea came into Arnav's mind.

"Hey remember that trap door in the graveyard, let's go and see what's inside." Arnav said with adrenaline rushing across his body. "But it's too late" Shubh replied although he was also too excited. "Don't be afraid let's go!" exclaimed Arnav.

As they entered the graveyard closing the gate quietly, they realised how frightening it was to wander in there at night. Both the brothers gained the courage and started walking dodging the thorny bushed and dried up thorny wooden sticks.

 In nearly a minute they came near the big tree and spotted the trapdoor. Shubh tried to open it but it didn't even move an inch, then both Arnav and Shubh mustered up all their power and pulled. Still, it made no difference. Panting and breathing heavily both the brothers went to their room to sleep.

Into the Trapdoor

In the dimly lit room of their hostel, the brothers lay in their beds, their earlier excitement still palpable in the air. The trapdoor in the graveyard loomed large in their minds, its mystery beckoning them even as their bodies demanded rest.

"You think we'll be able to open it tomorrow?" Shubh asked, breaking the silence that had settled between them.

Arnav turned to face his brother, his eyes reflecting the moonlight streaming through the small window. "I'm sure we can. Maybe we just need the right tools or something."

Shubh nodded, already lost in thought about their plan. "Yeah, we could bring some crowbars or maybe a big stick. We've got to find out what's underneath."

The anticipation of their next adventure made sleep elusive. The hours passed slowly as both boys tossed and turned, their minds filled with the possibilities of what lay beneath the trapdoor. Finally, exhaustion won, and they drifted into a restless sleep, their dreams tangled with visions of hidden chambers and ancient secrets.

The following morning, the sun rose with a gentle warmth that filled their room. Arnav and Shubh awoke with a renewed sense of purpose, eager to continue their exploration. They quickly dressed and grabbed a few items they thought might be useful: a sturdy flashlight, a crowbar they found in the storage room, and a large, sturdy stick.

As they made their way back to the graveyard, the sunlight made the eerie surroundings of the previous night seem more benign, but the brothers were still tinged with a sense of nervous excitement. They approached the big tree where the trapdoor lay hidden beneath layers of overgrown foliage and debris.

With the crowbar in hand, Arnav tried prying open the trapdoor once more. The metal creaked and groaned under the pressure, but it remained stubbornly shut. Shubh joined in, using all his strength, and together, they managed to get it slight opening.

"Come on, we're almost there!" Arnav encouraged Shubh, his voice filled with determination.

Finally, with one last combined effort, the trapdoor gave way with a loud clank. The brothers peered into the dark opening below. The flashlight's beam revealed a stone staircase descending into darkness.

"This is it," Shubh whispered, his voice trembling with a mix of fear and excitement. "Let's go down and see what's there."

They descended the stairs slowly, each step echoing off the stone walls. The air grew cooler and mustier as they went deeper. At the bottom of the stairs, they reached a small chamber lit by their flashlight.

The chamber was filled with old, dusty relics and cobwebs. A wooden chest sat in the center, its surface covered in intricate carvings that had faded over time. Arnav and Shubh exchanged amazed glances.

"Do you think this is it?" Shubh asked, his voice barely above a whisper.

"Only one way to find out," Arnav replied.

They approached the chest and managed to pry it open. Inside, they found a collection of old documents, a few coins, and what appeared to be a faded map. The brothers carefully examined the map, which showed the layout of their village and some markings indicating other hidden locations.

"This is incredible!" Arnav exclaimed. "We've got to show this to someone. Maybe there's more to discover."

Shubh nodded eagerly. "Definitely. But for now, let's make sure we're careful. We don't know what other surprises might be waiting for us."

With their newfound treasure and the thrill of discovery still fresh, the brothers made their way back up the stairs and sealed the trapdoor behind them. As they exited the graveyard, they couldn't stop talking about their next adventure and the possibilities that lay ahead.

The sun was high in the sky, casting a warm glow over their village. The brothers knew they had stumbled upon something special, and their summer was shaping up to be filled with excitement and exploration. They eagerly made plans to follow the map's clues, their minds buzzing with anticipation for what secrets the village—and its hidden history—might still hold.

After that, life returned to a semblance of normalcy, with everything going smoothly until the final two days before the summer holidays were set to begin.

The Sudden Attack

CRASHHH!!!!

The brothers were jolted awake by the deafening sound of shattering glass. Their room's window had been smashed, and a large stone lay on their study table, just inside the broken frame. They sprang from their beds and were confronted with a nightmarish scene that made their stomachs churn. The entire school was engulfed in flames, and the surrounding bushes in the graveyard were ablaze as well.

Outside, a mob of thirty to forty people brandished menacing banners reading "Bring us the demons" and "Sharma brothers will die." Police cars had arrived, but the officers struggled to control the chaotic situation. Terrified, Arnav and Shubh dared not venture outside. Instead, they scrambled to barricade their room by piling heavy furniture against the door, hoping to keep themselves safe from the turmoil outside.

The riot was eventually subdued by the police, but the damage was extensive. The next day, after the fire was extinguished and the smoke had cleared, the school walls were left blackened and charred. The Principal convened an urgent meeting with all students, informing them of the grim news: the school and hostel would require significant repairs due to the damage caused. Consequently, there would be an additional 15 days added to the summer holidays.

The students were instructed to vacate the hostel and find temporary housing in rented accommodations around the village, for which the local students would help them. The rapid sequence of events left the brothers in stunned silence, their earlier sense of stability shattered. The chaos and fear had driven a wedge between them, and they barely exchanged a word as they processed the shocking turn of events.

Shelter!

"We're supposed to vacate the hostel by 6:00 p.m.," Shubh said, glancing at the clock. "That means we need to start packing our things. It's already past five."

Arnav's voice trembled with anxiety. "Brother, why are they targeting us? We haven't done anything wrong. We've only been here for two months!"

Shubh placed a reassuring hand on Arnav's shoulder, trying to mask his own unease. "Don't worry, Arnav. We've faced challenges since the day we arrived, and we need to stay strong. We need to be prepared for anything, not by becoming aggressive, but by being vigilant. A small knife for self-defense might be wise. It's not about acting tough but about protecting ourselves. Now, let's hurry and pack up. We need to report to the ground floor quickly."

With a sense of urgency, the brothers began to gather their belongings, quickly stuffing clothes and personal items into their bags. The atmosphere was tense, the gravity of their situation pressing down on them as they worked swiftly. Despite Shubh's attempts to stay composed, both he and Arnav were deeply unsettled by the unfolding events.

When they finally joined the rest of the students in the crowded hallway, the chaos of the evacuation was palpable. The students, some still in shock, were being herded towards the exit. The brothers, along with the other students, made their way to the designated assembly point outside, where they were given directions to their temporary accommodations.

Arriving at the new rented houses scattered throughout the village, Arnav and Shubh saw the accommodations were far from ideal. There were not enough rooms for everyone to live separately, so the students were divided into ten groups, each consisting of four members. The atmosphere was one of weary resignation as the students adjusted to their new reality.

Arnav and Shubh found themselves sharing a room with two twelfth graders. The room was modest and somewhat cramped, but it offered a semblance of stability amid the chaos. The older students, though weary, greeted them with a mix of empathy and shared frustration. The brothers quickly realized that they would need to adapt to this new living arrangement and forge new relationships in the unfamiliar environment.

As the sun set and the first evening in their new homes began, the brothers settled into their room, trying to find a sense of normalcy. The uncertainty

of their situation and the looming
threat from the village left them
anxious, but they knew they had to
remain strong and support each
other through the challenges ahead.

Search for New Weapons!

The brothers, now settled into their
room with their new roommates,
tried to make sense of their situation.
The two twelfth graders, Nirmal and
Dhruv, seemed to be adjusting to the
sudden change with a mix of
resignation and curiosity.

Shubh broke the silence, his voice
laced with a hint of nervousness.
"Can I ask you something?"

Nirmal, looking up from his belongings, nodded. "Sure, go ahead."

"We need to find a place where we can buy a knife," Shubh said, trying to sound casual but failing to hide the urgency in his tone.

Dhruv, who had been quietly organizing his things, glanced up with a raised eyebrow. "A knife? Why do you need one?"

Arnav, sensing the need for full disclosure, added, "You know about the attack on the school, right?"

Nirmal and Dhruv exchanged a look of understanding. "Yes, we definitely

about it, that's why we are here"
Nirmal confirmed.

"That's because we are the Sharma brothers they were after," Shubh said, his face set in a serious expression. "We're concerned for our safety and believe it would be wise to have some form of protection."

Dhruv's eyes widened in shock. "You're the ones they were targeting? I had no idea. This is serious."

Arnav nodded. "Yes, and given the situation, we think it's important to have a means of defending ourselves. Do you know where we might be able to get a knife or something similar?"

Nirmal shook his head slowly. "Actually, the village doesn't really have many places where you can buy such things. It's not exactly the sort of place where weapons are readily available. Most people here rely on traditional methods and tools rather than anything more modern."

Dhruv sighed. "But we understand your concern. Even though the village lacks these types of supplies, we'll do what we can to help. We might know someone who has connections or might be able to find something through local networks. It's not guaranteed, but we'll try."

Nirmal nodded in agreement. "We'll start asking around and see if we can find anything. For now, stay cautious and keep your wits about you. This village may seem quiet, but it's clear there are some serious issues beneath the surface."

The brothers felt a mixture of relief and continued apprehension. While they were grateful for the offer of assistance, the reality of their situation was still daunting. They knew they needed to stay vigilant and adapt quickly to their new circumstances.

"Thank you," Shubh said, his voice filled with gratitude. "We really appreciate any help you can provide. We'll do our best to stay out of trouble and make the most of this situation."

Arnav added, "Yes, thank you. We'll try to keep a low profile and be as careful as we can."

Nirmal and Dhruv nodded, offering their support. As the evening wore on and the new roommates settled into their temporary home, the brothers tried to focus on their immediate needs, knowing that they were navigating a complex and uncertain path in this unfamiliar village.

Fort Runes

The excitement of their previous discovery, fueled Arnav and Shubh's enthusiasm as they prepared for their next adventure. Over the following days, they spent their free time studying the old map and researching the village's history to understand the significance of the markings they had found.

The map indicated a series of locations, each marked with cryptic symbols. One particular location caught their attention—a set of runes on the map pointed towards an area marked as "Fort Runes" situated deep in the forest to the east of their village.

As summer vacation approached, the brothers made detailed plans. They packed essential supplies: a compass, a first aid kit, some snacks, and a notebook for recording their findings. They also brought along their old flashlight, which had become their trusty companion on previous adventures.

The day of their expedition dawned clear and bright. The brothers set out early in the morning, their hearts pounding with anticipation. The forest was a sprawling maze of dense trees and underbrush, but the map provided a rough guide. With Arnav leading the way, they followed the map's directions, carefully navigating through the forest.

After several hours of trekking through the thick foliage, they reached a clearing. At the center stood the remains of what looked like a once-grand fort. Weathered stone walls and crumbling towers rose from the ground, partially obscured by creeping vines and overgrown vegetation.

"Wow, look at this!" Shubh exclaimed, his eyes wide with awe. "This must be Fort Runes!"

The brothers approached the fort cautiously. The entrance was partially blocked by fallen debris, but they managed to squeeze through. Inside, the air was cool and musty, and the light from their flashlights danced across the stone walls, revealing faded murals and ancient inscriptions.

They carefully explored the fort, noting the different rooms and passageways. One chamber contained old weapons and armours "Look at these, some old swords and knives!" Arnav exclaimed. ""We finally found what we needed," Shubh said, surveying the collection of knives they had gathered. "Let's take these with us. They might be rusty, but they could still be useful. They don't appear to be antiques or relics; they look like they've been here for only a short time." Shubh suggested. Another room had a series of runes carved into the walls, which matched the symbols on their map.

"This must be important," Arnav said, examining the runes closely. "These could be clues or part of some puzzle."

Shubh nodded in agreement. "Let's see if we can decode them. Maybe they'll lead us to something hidden."

The brothers set to work, using their notebook to sketch the runes and compare them to the symbols on their map. After some trial and error, they deciphered that the runes formed a sequence that pointed to a hidden compartment in the wall.

With careful effort, they pried open the compartment, revealing a small, intricately designed box. Inside the box, they found a collection of old scrolls and a key with an ornate design.

"These scrolls look like they might contain more information about the village's history," Shubh said, carefully unrolling one of them.

As they studied the scrolls, they discovered they contained detailed records of the village's founding, ancient battles, and legendary figures. The key appeared to be significant, but its purpose was unclear.

Excited by their findings, the brothers made their way back to the village, determined to uncover more about the key and its connection to their village's history. They visited the village historian, an elderly man named Mr. Kapoor, who had a vast knowledge of local lore and legends.

Mr. Kapoor examined the scrolls and the key with great interest. "These are remarkable," he said, his eyes twinkling with excitement. "The key is a part of a legend about a hidden vault beneath the village—rumoured to contain treasures and important artifacts from our ancestors."

Arnav and Shubh listened intently as Mr. Kapoor recounted tales of the hidden vault and the history behind it. He explained that the vault was said to be located somewhere beneath the village, accessible only through a series of hidden passages and clues.

"The map you found and the key you have may very well be the keys to uncovering this vault, but it seems there must be another key similar to this which we have and only with help of the two, we can open the treasure" Mr. Kapoor said. "If you wish, I can assist you in your search."

Kidnapped!

Several days had gone by since the upheaval they had experienced. Life had settled into a routine, and the intensity of their recent adventure had begun to fade into the background.

"Today's my turn to work at the timber yard," Arnav said as he tucked his newly acquired knife into his pocket. "I'm heading out now. See you later."

After a long day of cutting timber, Arnav was heading back to their new house. As he walked along the dimly lit street, he noticed something unusual. A figure in black robes, wearing a hat and a mask, was clambering up a ladder next to a row of street lights. The man seemed to be tampering with the lights, causing them to flicker and go out one by one on one side of the street, while the other side remained illuminated.

Arnav's curiosity and concern grew as he observed the scene. He could see the man working on the light directly in front of him, and he watched as the light went out completely. Instinctively, Arnav's hand went to the knife in his pocket. He unfolded it, the blade glinting in the fading light.

Summoning his courage, Arnav approached the man cautiously. "Hey, are you okay? What are you doing there?" he called out, trying to keep his voice steady.

The figure did not respond. Arnav took a few more steps closer and repeated his question, his voice tinged with increasing concern. "Hey, what's going on? Can you hear me?"

Still, there was no answer. The man, now appearing more agitated, took two deliberate steps down the ladder. Suddenly, with a surprising burst of energy, he leaped from the ladder, shoving it forcefully toward Arnav. The ladder clattered to the ground, narrowly missing Arnav.

Arnav's heart raced as he tried to make sense of the situation. The man's sudden and aggressive move left him on edge. Adrenaline surged through him as he tightened his grip on the knife, preparing for whatever might come next. The street, now

half dark and half lit, seemed to grow
eerily silent as the confrontation
unfolded.

Arnav barely had time to react before
the man lunged at him. The figure's
masked face was filled with
determination, and the robed
silhouette moved with alarming
speed. Arnav, knife in hand, tried to
defend himself but was taken aback
by the man's sudden aggression.

The man struck first, swinging a
gloved hand toward Arnav's face.
Arnav managed to dodge, but the
force of the swing caught him off
guard, making him stumble
backward. The man seized the
opportunity, lunging again with a low
kick aimed at Arnav's legs. Arnav
tried to block with his knife, but the
kick connected, knocking him off

balance and causing him to drop the blade.

Desperate, Arnav scrambled to retrieve the knife, but the man was relentless. He grabbed Arnav by the collar, lifting him off his feet and slamming him against the side of a nearby building. Arnav gasped in pain as the cold, rough wall pressed against his back. The man's grip was vice-like, and his strength seemed unnatural.

Arnav twisted and wriggled, trying to break free, but the man's hold was unyielding. With a sudden jerk, the man pulled Arnav away from the wall and slammed him down onto the ground. Arnav's head spun from the impact, and he struggled to focus as he tried to get up.

The man swiftly retrieved a length of rope from inside his robe and began to bind Arnav's hands behind his back. Arnav fought against the ropes, but they tightened with each attempt. His heart pounded as he realized the gravity of the situation. The streetlights flickered ominously, casting long shadows that danced across the scene.

As Arnav's hands were secured, the man pulled him to his feet and threw him over his shoulder. Arnav, dazed and disoriented, could barely see what was happening. The man moved with surprising agility, navigating the darkened street with Arnav in tow. The dim glow from the streetlights revealed glimpses of the man's determined expression, but not much else.

Arnav struggled to free himself, but the ropes were too tight. His mind raced as he tried to come up with a plan. The muffled sounds of the village seemed distant, swallowed by the encroaching darkness and the man's heavy breathing. As they continued down the street, Arnav saw the outlines of the houses and buildings blur past. Panic set in as he realized he was being taken further from safety.

Suddenly, the man veered off the main road and into a narrow, overgrown path. The foliage scraped against Arnav's legs as they moved deeper into the woods. Arnav tried to call out for help, but his voice was muffled by the man's shoulder and the thick fabric of his robe. The sound of his own struggle seemed to fade into the night, swallowed by the rustling leaves and the distant cries of nocturnal creatures.

After what felt like an eternity, the man finally emerged into a small clearing, where a dilapidated cabin stood in the shadows. The cabin looked abandoned, with broken windows and a sagging roof. The man approached the cabin, pushing open a creaky door with a forceful shove.

Inside, the cabin was dark and musty, filled with the smell of mildew and decay. The man carried Arnav to the center of the room and roughly dropped him onto the floor. Arnav winced as he hit the ground, his hands still bound and his body aching from the rough handling.

The man moved around the cabin, making adjustments to the surroundings as if preparing for something. Arnav, still trying to regain his composure, glanced around the room for anything he could use to free himself. The dim light from a single, flickering bulb cast eerie shadows across the walls.

Just as Arnav's eyes adjusted to the darkness, the man turned back toward him. His masked face was illuminated by the bulb's weak light, revealing a look of cold determination.

"Why are you doing this?" Arnav managed to ask, his voice hoarse. "What do you want from me?" and then he fainted.

The Search

It was already half past eight, Arnav didn't come back from his work. "Maybe he had been given some extra work to do" Shubh thought. For Shubh, the time was flowing quickly. It was now ten o-clock but still no sigh of Arnav. Shubh asked Dhruv if he'll accompany him to find Arnav but he was already on bed and wanted to sleep so he disagreed Shubh's idea wandering in the dark. He also told Shubh to look for Nirmal who had gone for a walk but still hadn't returned.

It was unusual for Arnav to be so late without any word, and a sinking feeling had settled in Shubh's stomach. He decided to investigate, hoping to find his brother and ensure everything was alright.

After retracing Arnav's path to the timber yard and speaking with some villagers, Shubh learned about the strange figure messing with the street lights. A sense of dread overwhelmed him as he realized that Arnav might be in serious trouble. He knew he had to act quickly.

Shubh, with his heart pounding, set out in the direction where Arnav had last been seen. He followed the trail of broken street lights and signs of disturbance. The path led him to the narrow, overgrown route that Arnav had been dragged down.

As Shubh navigated through the dense foliage and followed the trail of disrupted vegetation, he could hear the distant sounds of the night – rustling leaves, distant animal calls, and the occasional snap of a twig underfoot. The sounds of the forest seemed to amplify his anxiety as he pushed forward, determined to find his brother.

Eventually, Shubh arrived at the clearing and saw the dilapidated cabin in the distance. His heart sank as he approached the cabin cautiously. The sight of the old, sagging building, with its broken windows and eerie silence, confirmed his worst fears.

He crept up to the cabin, peeking through the gaps in the wooden planks. The flickering light from inside provided just enough illumination for

Shubh to see Arnav, bound and lying on the floor. The man in black robes was sitting in a chair, facing Arnav with a cold, menacing gaze.

Shubh's pulse quickened as he formulated a plan. He had to get inside without alerting the man. He quietly moved around the cabin, searching for a way in. After a tense few moments, he found a small, partially broken window at the back of the cabin. It was just big enough for him to squeeze through.

With careful precision, Shubh managed to pry the window open and climb inside. The cabin's interior was just as unsettling as it had seemed from the outside. He spotted Arnav immediately, but he also saw the man in the chair, who was now looking toward the door with an alert expression.

Shubh's plan was to sneak up on the man, overpower him, and free Arnav. He took a deep breath and moved silently across the room. He had a small wrench in his pocket that he planned to use as a weapon if necessary. He approached the man from behind, trying to stay as quiet as possible.

Just as Shubh was about to reach the man, his foot caught on a loose floorboard, causing it to creak loudly. The man's head snapped up, and he turned around with a menacing glare. Realizing he had been discovered, Shubh lunged at the man, but the man was ready.

The man quickly stood up and grabbed a nearby heavy object, swinging it toward Shubh. Shubh ducked and tried to dodge the blow, but the man's strength and speed were formidable. They engaged in a fierce struggle, with Shubh trying to land a few solid hits while the man retaliated with powerful, precise strikes.

Despite Shubh's best efforts, the man's superior strength and the element of surprise worked against him. The man managed to land a blow to Shubh's side, knocking the wind out of him. Dazed and disoriented, Shubh struggled to regain his footing, but the man took advantage of the opportunity.

With a swift move, the man disarmed Shubh and knocked him to the ground. Shubh tried to get up, but the man was relentless. He grabbed Shubh by the collar and threw him against the wall, pinning him down. Shubh's attempts to fight back were futile; he was overpowered and outmatched.

The man's footsteps grew louder as he approached Arnav. Shubh could barely see Arnav's face, but he could sense the fear emanating from his brother. The man knelt beside Arnav, inspecting the ropes that bound him, his movements deliberate and calculated.

Suddenly, the sound of shuffling footsteps reached Shubh's ears. The man's head snapped up, and his eyes narrowed as he listened intently. The footsteps grew louder, and it became clear that someone was approaching the cabin.

The man's demeanor shifted from focused to frantic. He glanced at Shubh and Arnav, his eyes filled with a mix of anger and panic. Without a word, he grabbed Arnav and lifted him from the floor, dragging him roughly toward the cabin's exit. Arnav, still bound and weak from the struggle, was powerless to resist.

Shubh struggled against his own restraints, trying to call out for help, but his voice was muffled by the ropes. His heart pounded with a mix of fear and anger as he watched helplessly. The sound of footsteps grew louder, and Shubh hoped against hope that the approaching figures were villagers coming to their rescue.

As the man hurriedly dragged Arnav outside, the door of the cabin burst open. A group of villagers, led by some of the older students from the school, stormed into the cabin. They had followed the trail of disturbance and the cries for help that Shubh had managed to make before he was overpowered.

The villagers immediately sprang into action, their faces set with determination. They quickly freed Shubh from his bindings, their hands working with practiced efficiency. Shubh, though relieved to be free, couldn't shake the feeling of dread as he realized the man had taken Arnav and was now escaping into the night.

"Where is he?" Shubh demanded, his voice urgent. "He took my brother! We have to go after him!"

One of the villagers, a grizzled man with a stern expression, nodded firmly. "We've already called for backup. The police are on their way, but we'll search for him in the meantime."

Shubh, still shaking off the remnants of his fear and pain, joined the villagers in their search. They split up, scouring the surrounding area for any sign of the man or Arnav. The darkness of the forest and the chaos of the night made the search difficult, but Shubh pushed on, driven by his concern for his brother.

"We'll definitely find him, but now you need rest" one the villager said.

In the Forest

Shubh was lying down on his mattress. Dhruv was sitting near the studying table, watching Shubh. It seemed Dhruv was lost in a deep thought. Shubh stood up and went to brush his teeth. When he came back, he asked Dhruv if he can get some food. "Sure, just wait a minute I'll give you the food which you forgot to eat last night" Dhruv said. Shubh said in desperation "Today I'll search for him in the forest". "I have a theory" Dhruv began "What if after work Arnav met Nirmal, then the man kidnapped both of them as he thought the second child was you?

But then he realised that it wasn't you, also he couldn't release Nirmal or he would tell us, so he captured him and also waited for you to come. Nirmal is missing too you were tired and injured last night so I didn't tell you this". "I don't know but, I only saw Arnav yesterday" Shubh said. "Why don't you inform the police?" Dhruv enquired. "Police will publicise the matter and the kidnapper will take him away. They want me and I'll definitely go there and show them who I am" Shubh said savagely. "Ok so today I'll accompany you to search for both of them" Dhruv told him. "No, I can't risk your life as well. I'll go and search the forest" Shubh told.

Shubh got dressed, putting his knife in his pocket. He was ready to go for the search again but this time fully prepared to kill any person who becomes his hinderance.

It was a very cloudy day and sun was hardly visible. It seemed as if it would rain heavily. "It will rain anytime now, see the clouds. You should wait for some time" Dhruv suggested, worrying for Shubh's health.

Shubh quickly ate a bread and went out. It was already raining, Dhruv was looking at Shubh disappointedly. "I've already searched the timber, the village and that house in the forest. Now, as I saw him going further towards the forest, I must go there" Shubh thought.

The moment he was about to reach there the rain was so fast that he could hardly see anything. The road was full of water covering his ankles. He took his knife out. He saw the forest ahead looked like as if it's trees were uprooted by a monster. Shubh's heart pounded as he fought against the relentless storm. The rain, now up to his waist, turned the forest floor into a treacherous swam. The cold water, driven by the wind, stung his skin as he struggled through the muddy terrain. Every step was a challenge, but the urgency to find Arnav kept him moving forward.

The forest was a chaotic blur of dark, swaying trees and swirling water. Shubh's knife, tightly gripped in his hand, was his only source of comfort. His mind raced with thoughts of his brother and the man who had taken him. The wind howled, and the rain battered him, but he pressed on, driven by fear and determination.

Suddenly, a flash of lightning illuminated the forest, briefly revealing a horrifying sight. Shubh's eyes widened as he saw a body hanging lifelessly from a tree. He squinted through the torrential downpour, and his heart sank as he realized it was Nirmal. The boy's lifeless form was eerily illuminated by the occasional flashes of lightning, his face a ghostly pallor in the storm's light.

Shubh froze, his breath catching in his throat. The sight of Nirmal's body was a crushing blow. He had hoped that Nirmal might be alive, but the stark reality of the scene was overwhelming. The body was bound and hung with ropes, a grim testament to the violence that had taken place. Shubh's stomach churned with dread and sorrow.

"No, no, no…" Shubh muttered to himself, struggling to keep his emotions in check. He couldn't afford to break down now. The thought of Arnav potentially meeting the same fate fueled his resolve. With renewed urgency, he quickly scanned the area around the tree, searching for any sign of Arnav or any clue that could help him find his brother.

Shubh suddenly felt mortal danger so he turned to go back then he heard a swift sound for a merely a second….

Sweeeeeep!!

Shubh scanned his surroundings, then realised what it was and dived into the water.

Two Dead

Shubh knew it was bullet, he realised he was going to die any moment. "Although the water would give me infections if I open my eyes, but what would I do with these eyes if I'll die?" Shubh thought. He opened his eyes and saw a bullet slowing down by the water very close to him. He quickly swam to the opposite direction, towards the entrance of the forest. As the water became shallow, he quickly ran towards a tree.

Sweeeeep!!

Before he could hide behind the tree, he was shot on his waist but still he quickly ran to the tree. He was feeling a very strong pain in his chest, his heart would burst, he thought. "This is my end, I couldn't save my brother, I failed..." Shubh thought. He ran his fingers through his waist and saw blood all over his fingers. "But I can't stop, I must save my brother, I can't die, for my brother's sake" Shubh resisted his negative thoughts. He waited there for some moments and realised the firing has stopped. "Maybe the attacker went away, thinking that I escaped from him, maybe he was afraid that someone could come to rescue me and catch him" Shubh thought and without further delay he quickly ran towards the entrance. As he reached there, he took a last look at Nirmal's dead body. The water on the road was shallower than that in forest, but then something happened due to which Shubh's stomach lurched and seemed like his heart would pop out from his mouth. A man wearing a black mask, covering his whole face, was standing in front of him, wearing a half pant and a torn half t-shirt. The man laughed loudly "Finally, finally, I'll get revenge, I'll get revenge for my master, he'll place me in his most trusted men! Ha! Ha! Ha! Ha! Ha! You've escaped many times from me. Although my master wanted you alive but because of your mischief, you'll dieee!" shouted the man taking his gun out. "One minute- just tell me is my brother alright? I don't wanna die without knowing about his wellness" Shubh cried, taking a step forward. "You're lucky, you'll die without much pain, but your brother...." The man couldn't complete his sentence as Shubh lunged over the man. His gun fell away from them and Shubh punched him as hard as he could on the face. The man reversed the positions and tried to suffocate Shubh by pressing his neck against the road.

Bang!

The grip over Shubh's neck became loose as the man fell down, splashing the water everywhere. Shubh quickly stood up and saw Saransh holding a pistol still aiming at the man. The man was dead, the bullet hit him on his head. "What were you doing here, are you mad" Saransh enquired. "Why did you shoot him? Now you're in big trouble" Shubh said shockingly. "If I hadn't killed him, it was you who would have been killed" Saransh said

"Now come with me, I'll take you to the village's doctor, you're losing a lot of blood. Press your hand against your wound but first I must see the bullet inside. If it's just on the outer layer of the skin I must remove it" Saransh advised. He came to Shubh and plucked the bullet out from his waist, he flinched. "You're lucky, the bullet hadn't gone so far as to infect you, you're safe, but now let's get to the doctor" Saransh said. "Why are you carrying this pistol with you?" Shubh asked. "It's not the time for questions, let's go" Saransh said, showing severity.

Interrogation

The morning sun filtered weakly through the clouds as the rain subsided, leaving the village with a damp, eerie stillness. The aftermath of the events had left everyone shaken, and the police were working tirelessly to piece together the details. The village square was abuzz with the presence of officers, their stern faces reflecting the gravity of the situation.

After Shubh got his treatment, he,
Saransh and Dhruv went to the police
station.

Shubh, his shirt stained with blood
and his movements pained, sat in a
modest office in the village's
makeshift police station. The room,
though functional, was small and
cluttered with papers and maps.
Saransh, his loyal friend, was beside
him, offering what support he could.
Dhruv, who had been anxiously
waiting outside, paced back and
forth.

Detective Rana, a seasoned
investigator with a reputation for
thoroughness, sat behind a cluttered
desk. His eyes, sharp and focused,
assessed Shubh with a mix of concern

and professionalism. Officer Mehta, a younger, diligent officer, stood by with a notepad, ready to record the details.

"Mr. Shubh," Detective Rana began, his voice calm but authoritative, "we need to get a clear account of what happened last night. This will help us understand the situation and locate your brother and any other victims involved."

Shubh nodded, his face pallid but determined. "Of course, Detective. I'll tell you everything I know."

Detective Rana gestured for Shubh to start, and Officer Mehta began to scribble notes.

"I had been searching for my brother, Arnav," Shubh began, his voice steady despite his exhaustion. "He didn't come home from work, which was unusual. I found out that he had been seen near the timber yard and then down a path towards the forest."

"Did anyone see him leaving the timber yard?" Detective Rana asked, leaning forward slightly.

"Yes," Shubh confirmed. "Some villagers saw him heading in that direction. There was also a report about a suspicious figure tampering with streetlights. I think that man might have been involved."

"Alright," Detective Rana said, nodding. "Please continue."

Shubh took a deep breath. "I followed the trail into the forest. It was raining heavily. As I pushed through the forest, I found Nirmal's body hanging from a tree. It was a shock. I knew then that the situation was dire. I had barely had a chance to process this when I heard a gunshot. I was hit in the waist and took cover behind a tree."

Detective Rana's eyes narrowed. "Did you see the shooter?"

Shubh hesitated before answering. "Yes, I saw him just before I was shot.

He was wearing a black mask and had a gun. He seemed to be after me, not Arnav specifically. He mentioned something about revenge and his master. He was prepared to kill me."

"And then?" Detective Rana prodded.

"I managed to escape and was found by Saransh," Shubh said. "He arrived just in time to save me. He shot the man who was attacking me."

"Do you know why the kidnapper wanted revenge?" Detective Rana asked, his curiosity piqued.

"No," Shubh admitted. "He never explained. But he seemed to have been waiting for me and wanted to take revenge for some past event."

"But where is Nirmal's body?" Detective Rana asked looking towards other officers. "We didn't find anyone, sir" one of the officers replied.

 Detective Rana said "The killer might have taken him". He then glanced at Officer Mehta, who continued to take notes. "We need to know everything about the man in the mask. Did he say anything else?"

"Not much," Shubh said, shaking his head. "He mentioned his master and seemed angry."

Detective Rana leaned back in his chair, contemplating. "And where is Arnav now?"

"I don't know," Shubh replied, his voice heavy with worry. "I was too injured to continue searching after Saransh found me. The search party was out all night looking for him. I hope they've had better luck."

Detective Rana turned to Officer Mehta. "Prepare a detailed report of everything Mr. Shubh has mentioned. We need to track down any information related to this man's master and the motives behind these attacks."

Officer Mehta nodded and began typing up the notes.

"Mr. Shubh," Detective Rana said, turning back to him, "we will do everything we can to find your brother and investigate this matter further. Your information is crucial. If you remember anything else, please contact us immediately."

Shubh nodded, his resolve unshaken despite his injuries. "Thank you, Detective. I just want my brother back."

As the interrogation concluded, Saransh helped Shubh out of the office. Dhruv joined them, his face a mix of relief and concern. They stepped into the cool morning air, the rain leaving a fresh scent in the atmosphere. The village was still in turmoil, but the hope of finding Arnav and unravelling the mystery behind the man in the mask remained strong.

Detective Rana watched them leave, deep in thought. The case was far from over, and the stakes were high. He knew that every detail, every lead, would be critical in bringing Arnav back safely and uncovering the truth behind the night's chilling events.

Sneaking

Shubh and Dhruv had spent the past few days in silence, a numbing routine of sleeping, eating, and sleeping again, as if retreating into the quiet darkness of their thoughts. The events that had transpired were too overwhelming to process in the light of day. Saransh had been caught by the police, found with a pistol hidden in his bag, the same one used in the horrific events that had taken place. The school, now stained with the weight of tragedy, had shut down its classes for fifteen more days, as if trying to escape the eerie shadow that loomed over it.

It was during one of these nights that
Shubh finally broke down, the dam
holding his emotions back shattered.
"You know, I suffered a lot that day,"
Shubh whispered, his voice trembling
as he stared blankly at the wall. His
body seemed to shake with the
memory. "When I was shot, it
drained everything I had just to keep
moving, to escape. And then...
Nirmal... seeing him hanging there...
it... it was too much... too much..."
His voice cracked as tears streamed
down his face. The image of Nirmal's
lifeless body haunted him, playing on
a loop in his mind like a twisted
nightmare.

Dhruv, sitting on the edge of his bed,
sighed deeply, running a hand
through his messy hair. "We can't do

anything now, Shubh. It's over. Everything's over. I lost my friend. You... you lost your...," he trailed off, struggling to find the right words to console his friend. There was no comfort to offer.

"No!" Shubh's voice rang out sharply, startling Dhruv. His eyes were wide, desperate. "I haven't lost Arnav yet! I'll find him! I'll continue my search!" he shouted, his voice filled with determination, the tears still fresh on his cheeks.

Dhruv's frustration bubbled to the surface, unable to hold back any longer. "Are you mad? The police are already investigating to find him! And you were told not to leave, to stay put. You're going to get yourself killed!" Dhruv's voice raised in exasperation, trying to reason with Shubh, who seemed to be spiraling deeper into his own mission.

Shubh shook his head, burying his face in his hands. "No, the police aren't doing anything. They're not even looking in the right place. I keep a regular check from the terrace. Not once have I seen any of them near the forest. They're ignoring it!" His voice cracked, filled with both anger and helplessness.

Dhruv stood in silence for a moment, then sighed, pulling his blanket tighter around his shoulders as the cold night air seeped through the open window. "Well... it's already 10 p.m. There's nothing we can do tonight. Let's just hope Arnav comes back safely... but for now, we need rest," he muttered, his voice weary. He lay back on his bed, pulling the blanket over his head, trying to block out both the chill and the overwhelming tension in the room.

Shubh, still shaken, closed the window, trying to shut out the cold. He sat on his bed for a few moments longer, staring at the moonlight that filtered weakly through the thin curtains. It was the only light in the room, casting faint shadows that danced on the walls. Eventually, he lay down, closing his eyes, though sleep seemed far away.

Crack!!

The sound shattered the stillness of the night, echoing through the room. Both Shubh and Dhruv jolted awake instantly, their hearts pounding in their chests. The sharp noise came from the window. They stared in horror as they saw a large hand, dirty and calloused, trying to pull off the grill from the window. The glass was already shattered, pieces of it glimmering ominously on the floor inside the room. The dark shape of the figure outside loomed, massive and threatening.

It was too dark to see much of anything clearly, except for the faint outline of the study table that caught a dim sliver of moonlight. Shubh's breath hitched in his throat as he leapt out of bed, his adrenaline pumping. Without a second thought, he grabbed the knife from the study table and positioned himself in front of the window, his hands trembling as the intruder continued to rip the grill apart.

The students in the neighboring rooms had already woken up, alarmed by the noise, and began gathering outside the door. The tension was suffocating. The man outside didn't speak, but he suddenly thrust his hand inside, reaching for Shubh, who instinctively stepped back, clutching the knife tighter.

The man seemed to realize he was on the verge of being caught. With a sudden, swift motion, he let go of the grill and jumped back from the window. Shubh and Dhruv rushed to the window just in time to catch a glimpse of the enormous figure retreating into the shadows, disappearing into the darkness beyond the building.

"I think... I think I recognize him," Shubh whispered, his voice barely audible. His mind raced as he tried to place the familiarity of the figure.

Dhruv, still catching his breath, nodded in agreement, his face pale. "Yeah... he looked like someone we know... but who?" His voice trailed off as the realization began to dawn on both of them, though neither wanted to voice their thoughts.

As the other students piled into their room, drawn by the commotion, Shubh and Dhruv exchanged a silent glance. They didn't tell the others everything, only mentioning that someone had tried to break in, keeping the full truth about the figure to themselves. It felt too dangerous to reveal what they suspected.

After the crowd dispersed and the room was somewhat calm again, Dhruv turned to Shubh, his voice low and strained. "What do you think is happening? I mean... you don't reckon you're part of some gang from where you come from, do you?"

Shubh shook his head quickly. "No... I'm just a normal kid from Jabalpur. My grandparents sent me here...," he began, then suddenly paused, as if a realization had struck him. "Wait... my grandparents... no... my parents... they've got something to do with this place. The village people... they know my father."

Dhruv raised an eyebrow. "You never told me that. You knew your father lived here?"

Shubh swallowed hard, shaking his head. "No. I didn't know."

The room was silent for a moment, the weight of Shubh's words hanging heavily between them. Finally, Dhruv let out a long, frustrated sigh. "You know what? It's too much. This whole thing... I can't do it anymore. I can't

put my life in danger like this." His
voice wavered, filled with both fear
and exhaustion.

Shubh turned to him, confused. "So?"

"I'm leaving this room," Dhruv said,
his voice firmer now, though still
tinged with uncertainty. "I'm sorry,
but... I can't stay here anymore. I'm
done." Dhruv's voice broke slightly at
the end, his emotions overwhelming
him. He was speechless, torn
between loyalty to his friend and the
growing fear that had taken root in
his heart.

The Final Night

After Dhruv left, the room felt emptier than ever. Shubh was left to grapple with the suffocating weight of his thoughts. The silence around him was overwhelming, pressing down like a heavy blanket. Tears welled up in his eyes, and before he could stop them, they rolled down his cheeks. The memory of his brother Arnav brought fresh waves of sorrow, and the thought of Nirmal's death was unbearable. It wasn't just the tragedies of his friends that tore him apart, but the cumulative weight of fear, loss, and loneliness. Nothing in his life made sense anymore.

Days passed in a blur. School had resumed, but it felt like a cruel mockery of the normalcy that once was. Shubh walked to school alone each day, the quiet streets echoing his solitude. The familiar hallways now seemed alien, stripped of comfort. Classes became torture. His mind wandered incessantly, unable to focus. His studies, once a welcome distraction, now felt meaningless. No matter how hard he tried, thoughts of Arnav and Nirmal persisted.

School became a place of dread. Teachers, noticing his inattentiveness, began to single him out. During math class one particularly bad day, his teacher's frustration turned into anger.

"What's wrong with you? Can't you

pay attention for five minutes?" the teacher shouted. The embarrassment of being scolded in front of the entire class made Shubh's heart sink. Classmates stared, some whispering, others laughing. He felt their judgment, and it burned.

That Saturday night, as Shubh sat at his desk near the window, trying to finish his homework, exhaustion weighed heavily on him. It wasn't just the physical tiredness from school but the emotional toll of everything. He glanced at the clock: 8 p.m. He had promised himself he would be in bed by 9, hoping sleep might offer some reprieve. The words in his notebook blurred as his focus waned. Memories of Nirmal's lifeless body haunted him, the cold, empty expression forever etched in his mind.

A deep sigh escaped him as he tried to shake off the thoughts. But before he could return to his homework, a blood-curdling scream pierced the quiet night, chilling him to his core. The scream was raw with terror, echoing through the stillness and bouncing off the narrow street outside. Shubh's heart stopped, then raced as if trying to escape his chest. His hand froze mid-air, the pen rolling off the desk and clattering to the floor. Panicked, he rushed to the window, pulling the curtains aside.

The scene outside was surreal. A bright, unnaturally green light bathed the street in an eerie glow. The light was constant, casting distorted shadows. Driven by fear and curiosity, Shubh threw on his slippers and darted out of his room, rushing down the stairs and slamming the front door behind him. He sprinted towards the source of the light, his breath fogging in the cool night air.

When he reached the street, the scene before him made him stop dead in his tracks. The green light illuminated a figure, obscured by its brightness. Shubh squinted, trying to make out the shape, but the figure remained blurred, as if the light itself was hiding it. He gasped, drawing attention from the crowd that had gathered. Among them, he saw villagers and others staring in shock.

A man held something in his hand, and a person knelt on the stone floor of what looked like a huge lighthouse at the end of the forest. Shubh's heart skipped a beat as he recognized the figure on the ground.

"Arnav!!" Shubh screamed, his voice filled with desperation. The voice from a megaphone cut through the chaos, "You can save this child only if Shubh comes here within thirty minutes. Otherwise, he'll be found at the bottom of the lake by morning."

"Nooo!! I'm coming!" Shubh shouted back, his voice cracking. Determined, he ran towards the forest with all the speed he could muster, a knife tucked in his pocket. "This time, I'm fully prepared. I'll rescue my brother, even if it costs me my life," he thought, focused and resolute.

Navigating through the forest, Shubh's path was driven by sheer willpower. Finally reaching the lighthouse, he darted across the ramp and began climbing the stairs, knife in hand, every step fueled by urgency. At the top, he pushed open the door, revealing Arnav, kneeling and crying, and a large figure in a black robe and mask.

Shubh's blood ran cold. The man's build resembled the intruder from the hostel, but it was the face beneath the mask that left him in shock. "Nirmal?! You... You were dead! Someone killed you in the forest! How can you be here?"

Shubh's voice was filled with disbelief, his mind racing faster than he could process.

The man removed his mask... What Shubh said was true, it was Nirmal.

"How?" Shubh stammered, eyes wide in disbelief. "Do you think my master would kill his own supporter?" Nirmal sneered, gripping a pistol in his hand.

"You? A servant? Of who?" Shubh couldn't make sense of the situation.

"Saransh," Nirmal said with pride, "He's the almighty, greatest of all. You've no idea how well he treats his followers." Nirmal's tone shifted, a wicked grin spreading across his face. "But to his enemies? He's a nightmare. There's nothing he won't do to destroy them."

"Saransh?" Shubh's mind reeled. "But he saved me!"

Nirmal's laugh echoed through the lighthouse. "Saved you? Oh, Shubh, you're so naïve. That was all part of his plan".

Shubh's grip on his knife loosened, and it clattered to the floor.

"But if he wanted me dead, why did he kill the man who was about to do it?" Shubh's voice wavered, confusion clouding his thoughts.

Nirmal's eyes darkened. "That man would've given you a quick, painless death. Saransh doesn't want that. He wants you to suffer. That traitor wanted to spare you the agony, so Saransh killed him. And now, you'll know a pain far worse. You'll be dragged to the heart of the forest, and what happens next is beyond your worst nightmares."

"Why us?" Shubh blurted out, desperate for answers. "We haven't done anything to him. He attacked us on the first day—why?"

Nirmal's gaze narrowed, a sinister smile curling his lips. "Because of… your parents." He lunged at Shubh.

Instinct took over. Shubh dodged and crouched low, grabbing Nirmal's legs. With a grunt, Nirmal's chest slammed against the railing. Shubh stood up in a panic, and before he could think, he saw Nirmal teetering at the edge.

With a desperate kick, Shubh sent Nirmal tumbling over. For a brief moment, there was silence—then a sickening thud as Nirmal's body crashed onto the ramp below. Blood pooled around him, seeping from every part of his motionless form.

"No, no, no…" Shubh whispered in horror, backing away. "I killed him. I killed him. What have I done? What about Arnav…?"

Snapping out of his shock, Shubh turned to see Arnav still tied up, watching everything unfold in stunned silence. Shubh ran over, untying the ropes with trembling hands.

"Arnav, we need to go. Now!" Shubh hugged him quickly, pulling him to his feet. "The police will be here any second."

They rushed down the lighthouse stairs, Shubh's heart pounding as they reached the body. He noticed something—the bulge under Nirmal's cloak. A bag. Shubh grabbed it, then turned to Arnav. "Come on, follow me. I'll explain everything later."

The two of them fled toward the mountains, away from the village.

"We need to climb," Shubh panted. "The police won't follow us up there."

As they scrambled up the rocky slope, Arnav spotted a cave hidden at the farthest point of the mountain. He pointed it out to Shubh, and they made their way inside, catching their breath and looking out at the vast wilderness below.

The cave was surprisingly spacious, large enough to comfortably house ten people. Its high ceilings and wide expanse gave them a sense of shelter and safety. Exhausted, Shubh and Arnav made their way to the farthest corner and sank down, their backs

against the cool, rough stone, finally
allowing themselves a moment to
catch their breath.

Outlaws

"Bro, we're in serious trouble," Arnav said, his voice trembling as tears welled in his eyes. "First Saransh's gang, and now the police... it's too much."

Shubh placed a reassuring hand on his shoulder. "I know, Arnav. But panicking won't help us now. We need to stay strong. There's nothing we can do to change the situation, except to be smart about it. We'll hide here until things calm down. From this moment, we're like outlaws, just like Robin Hood and his gang."

Arnav's eyes widened. "You mean we're staying here... for how long?"

"As long as it takes," Shubh said firmly. "We'll sneak back to the hostel to grab our stuff, buy enough food to last a week, and lay low. We can't let anyone know we're here, not even the villagers. If they suspect anything, we'll be caught for sure."

With that, Shubh rummaged through the bag of the person who had betrayed them. "Let's see what this traitor was carrying... A laptop! But it's completely busted. And a phone... No, we can't turn this on; they could track us in seconds if we did."

His hand froze as he pulled out a folded piece of paper. "Wait... a map?" Shubh unfolded it carefully, studying the markings. "Look, there's a cross drawn right where the Fort Ruins is located! Could this be another treasure? Or maybe... the key, similar to the one we found? But it doesn't matter now"

Shubh stood, deep in thought. "There is one more thing, remember what Nirmal said—we're in danger because of something our parents did. How does all this connect to them? Sure, the villagers know our parents, but they couldn't have done something so terrible that we're now in mortal danger... could they?" Arnav asked.

Shubh sighed, trying to piece it all together. "We don't have all the answers yet. But for now, let's rest. We've been through hell today, and we need our strength for whatever comes next."

Arnav nodded, feeling a bit calmer now. "Yeah, you're right."

Shubh stretched out and gave Arnav a small smile. "Good night, Arnav. Tomorrow we'll figure this out."

As the quiet of the night enveloped them, Arnav mumbled sleepily, "Good night," before drifting into uneasy dreams.

Wait for part 2 to know about further mysteries like-

- What Shubh and Arnav's parents did
- What happened to Arnav that day when he was kidnapped
- The treasure hunt…….. and many more!!